AFTER HAPPILY EVER AFTER

Red Riding Hood Takes Charge

First published in the United States in 2009
by Stone Arch Books
151 Good Counsel Drive, P.O. Box 669
Mankato, Minnesota 56002
www.stonearchbooks.com

First published by Orchard Books, a division of Hachette Children's Books.
338 Euston Road, London NW1 3BH, United Kingdom

Library of Congress Cataloging-in-Publication Data
Bradman, Tony.
 Red Riding Hood Takes Charge / by Tony Bradman; illustrated by
Sarah Warburton.
  p. cm. — (After Happily Ever After)
  ISBN 978-1-4342-1308-2 (library binding)
  [1. Grandmothers—Fiction.] I. Warburton, Sarah, ill. II. Title.
PZ7.B7275Red 2009
[Fic]—dc22   2008031837

Summary: Little Red Riding Hood is worried about her Granny. Granny's
recovered from her scare with the Big Bad Wolf, but she's lonely. Thankfully
Little Red Riding Hood is on the case! She is ready to find her Granny some
new hobbies and some new friends.

Creative Director: Heather Kindseth
Graphic Designer: Emily Harris

                1 2 3 4 5 6 14 13 12 11 10 09

           Printed in the United States of America

AFTER

HAPPILY EVER AFTER

Red Riding Hood Takes Charge

by Tony Bradman

illustrated by Sarah Warburton

BILLINGS COUNTY PUBLIC SCHOOL
Box 307
Medora, North Dakota 58645

STONE ARCH BOOKS
www.stonearchbooks.com

So Little Red Riding Hood
and her Granny lived
happily ever after.
And then …

Little Red Riding Hood headed
down the woodland path, a basket
of cupcakes in one hand and a bunch
of flowers in the other.

It would be her first visit to Granny's for a while, and she hoped everything was okay. After all, it wasn't long since their scary incident with the Big Bad Wolf.

If it hadn't been for that nice man, Mr. Woodcutter, Little Red Riding Hood hated to think what might have happened.

She felt guilty too. Anyone else would probably have realized what the Big Bad Wolf was up to. But she hadn't, and Granny had almost paid a terrible price for her mistake.

Little Red Riding Hood sighed and told herself to be a lot more careful in the future.

"Who's that?" Granny called out when Little Red Riding Hood knocked on the cottage door. "You'll have to show me some ID!"

"It's all right, Granny," said Little Red Riding Hood. "It's me!"

Granny was pleased to see her and gave her a big hug and kiss.

"How are you?" asked Granny. "Is everything okay at school?"

"I'm fine," said Little Red Riding Hood. "But how are you?"

"Oh, I'm all right," said Granny. "Although I have to admit I do sometimes get a bit lonely out here."

"Lonely?" said Little Red Riding Hood.

"Did I say lonely?" laughed Granny.
"Don't worry, sweetheart, I'm all right.
Mmm, these cupcakes are delicious,
aren't they?"

Later that afternoon, Little Red Riding Hood trudged home, feeling guiltier than ever.

She should have realized Granny was lonely. Granny didn't have any neighbors, and Mom and Little Red Riding Hood lived too far away to visit her often.

"Hello there, Little Red Riding Hood!" a voice roared suddenly. A large, hairy figure appeared beside her.

"Yikes!" she squeaked. "Oh hi, Mr. Woodcutter. Sorry, you startled me."

"No problem," he boomed, smiling at her. He was a big man with a big beard. He was about the same age as Granny.

"Just been to see your Granny?" he asked. "How is she?"

"Well, mostly okay," said Little Red Riding Hood. Then she told him what Granny had said.

"A wonderful woman like your Granny feeling lonely?" he said. "I can hardly believe it! I would have thought she'd have plenty of visitors."

"Still, we are rather isolated in this part of the forest. I get lonely myself sometimes. Maybe I could stop over and see her," he added.

"Don't worry, Mr. Woodcutter," said
Little Red Riding Hood. "It's kind of
you to offer, but I'm sure I can think of
something. Anyway, I'd better be getting
home now. Goodbye!"

That evening, Little Red Riding Hood
sat in her room feeling bad. She would
just have to visit Granny more often. But
that might not be easy. There was hardly
a day when she didn't do something
after school.

The next day, Little Red Riding Hood thought she could get to Granny's and still be back in time for swimming.

Granny was surprised, but pleased, of course. And she seemed even more pleased when Little Red Riding Hood told her about the woodcutter.

"He asked about me?" said Granny, patting her hair. "Did he really?"

Little Red Riding Hood couldn't stay long. She hurried back, but she was late for swimming.

She went to see Granny the next day,
and the next, and the day after.

And she was late for her piano lesson and karate.

And she nearly missed Brownies.

There was another problem too. Little Red Riding Hood was running out of things to talk to Granny about.

"Cheer up, Little Red Riding Hood!" somebody roared. She jumped, but she knew it was only Mr. Woodcutter.

"Why the sad face?" he asked. Little Red Riding Hood explained what was worrying her now.

"I'm sure Granny loves seeing you, whatever you talk about," said the woodcutter.

"Maybe your Granny could do
with company her own age from time
to time, someone she's got more in
common with, someone like . . ."

"You might be right," said Little Red
Riding Hood before he could finish what
he was going to say. "It's worth a try,
anyway! Goodbye!"

That evening, Little Red Riding Hood searched The Forest Web and found something that looked promising. She signed Granny up for it.

"The club is called The Forest Belles, Granny," she said on her next visit. "And it's for people just like you—older ladies who live on their own. They meet twice a week and go on great trips. I bet you'll love it!"

But Granny didn't. She hated it and
stopped going after a week.

"I'm sorry, sweetheart," she said, "but being with a bunch of old ladies isn't my cup of tea. I mean, all they did was gossip and complain."

Little Red Riding Hood trudged homeward down the woodland path, even more worried than ever. She bumped into the woodcutter again.

"I see things aren't going well," he boomed.

Little Red Riding Hood explained about The Forest Belles.

"Can't say I blame Granny for feeling that way," said Mr. Woodcutter. "Sounds to me as if she'd prefer the company of one person. I could always . . ."

"I don't know, Mr. Woodcutter," Little Red Riding Hood said gloomily. "It would have to be the right person, but who could that be?" The woodcutter smiled broadly at her, but she didn't notice.

"You do have a point, though," she said. "Thanks for the advice. Goodbye!"

Mr. Woodcutter's shoulders sagged, and he sadly turned away.

That evening, Little Red Riding Hood checked The Forest Web again. She soon found something else that looked promising.

"It's called Forest Speed Dating, Granny," she said on her next visit. "They even have a Senior Citizens Night at the Palace Community Center. You'll meet lots of nice people, maybe even somebody special."

But Granny didn't. She hated it even more than The Forest Belles.

"I'm sorry, sweetheart," she said, "but I'd rather spend more time with just one person at a time. Then we can get to know each other."

That evening Little Red Riding Hood was filled with gloom. What else could she do?

She trudged home through the forest, and there was Mr. Woodcutter. He asked about Granny, and they chatted for a while. Then he sighed.

"Well, I'd better go," he said. "Oh, I meant to tell you. I'm thinking of moving away to start a new life somewhere else."

"Really? How wonderful!" said Little Red Riding Hood. "Well I ought to be getting home myself. All the best, Mr. Woodcutter. Goodbye!"

She walked down the path, thinking about Granny. And suddenly the answer hit her. She had known the right person all along—Mr. Woodcutter! Why hadn't she seen it before?

She frowned when she thought of how she ignored him each time he offered to visit Granny.

And now he was planning to move away and take Granny's chance of happiness with him. Little Red Riding Hood decided she wasn't going to ruin things for Granny again!

So the next day, there was a knock on Mr. Woodcutter's door. He was surprised to see Little Red Riding Hood.

"Hi, Mr. Woodcutter," she said. "I'm on my way to visit Granny, and I wondered if you'd like to come. I'm sure she'd love to see you!"

Mr. Woodcutter smiled. "I thought you'd never ask," he said.

Granny and Mr. Woodcutter got
along so well that within a month, they
announced they were getting married.

It was a wonderful wedding.
Little Red Riding Hood was Granny's
bridesmaid.

There was even a picture on the front page of *The Forest Times*.

And Granny and Mr. Woodcutter and
Little Red Riding Hood really did live
HAPPILY EVER AFTER!

THE END

ABOUT THE AUTHOR

Tony Bradman writes for children of all ages.
He is particularly well known for his top-selling
Dilly the Dinosaur series. His other titles include
the Happily Ever After series, The Orchard Book
of Heroes and Villains, and The Orchard Book of
Swords, Sorcerers, and Superheroes. Tony lives in
South East London.

ABOUT THE ILLUSTRATOR

Sarah Warburton is a rising star in children's
books. She is the illustrator of the Rumblewick
series, which has been very well received at an
international level. The series spans across both
picture books and fiction. She has also illustrated
nonfiction titles and the Happily Ever After series.
She lives in Bristol, England, with her young baby
and husband.

GLOSSARY

complain (kuhm-PLAYN)—to say something is wrong

gloom (GLOOM)—sadness

gossip (GOSS-ip)—to talk about other people

guilty (GIL-tee)—feeling bad for doing something wrong

incident (IN-suh-dent)—an event

isolated (EYE-suh-late)—set apart from others

startled (STAR-tuhld)—scared

trudged (TRUHJD)—walked slowly

woodland (WUD-luhnd)—a forest

DISCUSSION QUESTIONS

1. Granny lives in the middle of the woods with no neighbors. What kind of neighborhood do you live in? Do you have a lot of neighbors?

2. Granny is lonely. And after the wolf incident, she's also a little scared. Have you ever felt lonely or scared?

3. Mr. Woodcutter talks to Little Red Riding Hood every day, but she doesn't really listen to what he is saying. Discuss a time when you didn't listen.

WRITING PROMPTS

1. Little Red Riding Hood thinks of a lot of fun activites for her Granny. Make a list of five things that would be fun to do with a grandparent.

2. Little Red Riding Hood thinks her Granny should start dating. Write an ad describing the type of guy Granny would like to date.

3. At the end of the book, Granny and Mr. Woodcutter get married. *The Forest Times* newspaper runs a picture from the wedding. Write an article about the wedding to go with the picture.

Before there was **HAPPILY EVER AFTER**,
there was **ONCE UPON A TIME** …

Read the **ORIGINAL** fairy tales in **NEW** graphic novel retellings.

INTERNET SITES

Do you want to know more about subjects
related to this book? Or are you interested
in learning about other topics? Then check
out FactHound, a fun, easy way to find
Internet sites.

Our investigative staff has already sniffed
out great sites for you!

Here's how to use FactHound:

1. Visit *www.facthound.com*

2. Select your grade level.

3. To learn more about subjects related to
   this book, type in the book's ISBN number:
   1434213080.

4. Click the Fetch It button.

FactHound will fetch the best Internet sites for you!